Cool Duck

and

Lots of Hats

'Cool Duck' and 'Lots of Hats'
An original concept by Elizabeth Dale
© Elizabeth Dale

Illustrated by Giusi Capizzi

Published by MAVERICK ARTS PUBLISHING LTD

Studio 3A, City Business Centre, 6 Brighton Road,

Horsham, West Sussex, RH13 5BB

© Maverick Arts Publishing Limited May 2017

+44 (0)1403 256941

A CIP catalogue record for this book is available at the British Library.

ISBN 978-1-84886-249-4

www.maverickbooks.co.uk

Pink

This book is rated as: Pink Band (Guided Reading)
This story is decodable at Letters and Sounds Phase 2.

Cool Duck

and

Lots of Hats

By
Elizabeth Dale

Illustrated by
Giusi Capizzi

The Letter D

Trace the lower and upper case letter with a finger. Sound out the letter.

Around,
up,
down

Down,
up,
around

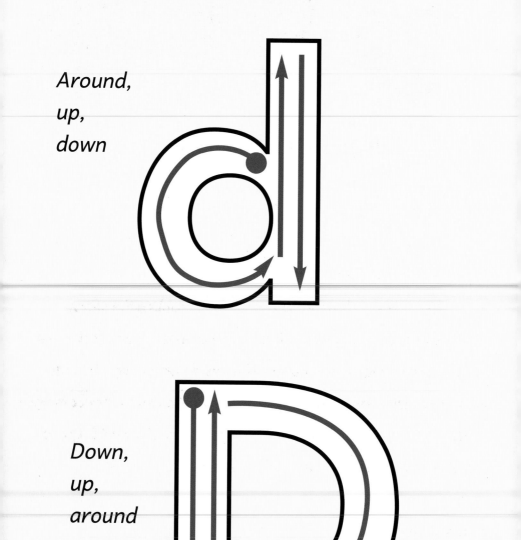

Some words to familiarise:

hot   splash   duck

High-frequency words:

the   is

Tips for Reading 'Cool Duck'

- Practise the words listed above before reading the story.

- If the reader struggles with any of the other words, ask them to look for sounds they know in the word. Encourage them to sound out the words and help them read the words if necessary.

- After reading the story, ask the reader why Cat and Dog are not hot or fed up at the end of the story.

Fun Activity

Discuss all the different things you can do to keep cool.

Cool Duck

The cat is hot.

The duck is cool.

The dog is hot.

Splash!

The dog is cool.

The cat is cool.

The duck is cool!

The Letter H

Trace the lower and upper case letter with a finger. Sound out the letter.

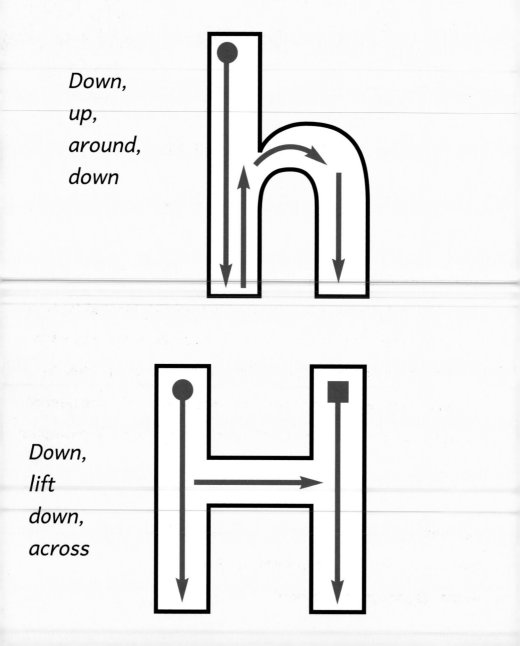

Down, up, around, down

Down, lift down, across

Some words to familiarise:

dog · hat · big

High-frequency words:

has of a the

Tips for Reading 'Lots of Hats'

- Practise the tricky words listed above before reading the story.
- If the reader struggles with any of the other words, ask them to look for sounds they know in the word. Encourage them to sound out the words and help them read the words if necessary.
- After reading the story, ask the reader why Pip ends up with all the hats.

Fun Activity

How many types of hat can you think of?

When do you wear each one?

Lots of Hats

Sam has a big hat.

Come back, hat.

Dad has a big, **big** hat.

Mum has a big, big, **big** hat.

The dog has lots of hats!

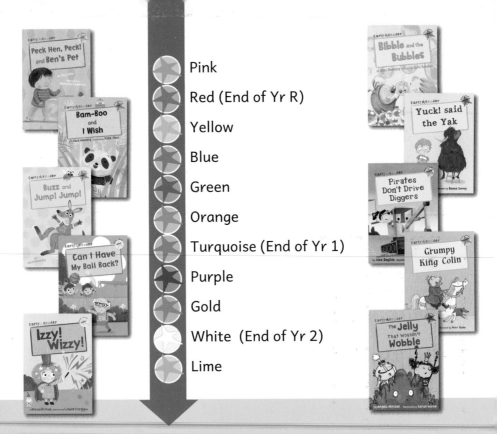

Pink

Red (End of Yr R)

Yellow

Blue

Green

Orange

Turquoise (End of Yr 1)

Purple

Gold

White (End of Yr 2)

Lime

Book Bands for Guided Reading

The Institute of Education book banding system is made up of twelve colours, which reflect the level of reading difficulty. The bands are assigned by taking into account the content, the language style, the layout and phonics.

Children learn at different speeds but the colour chart shows the levels of progression with the national expectation shown in brackets. To learn more visit the IoE website: www.ioe.ac.uk.

All of these books have been book banded for guided reading to the industry standard and edited by a leading educational consultant.

For more titles visit: www.maverickbooks.co.uk/early-readers